To:

From:

To my beautiful children who are my sun, my moon, and all my stars. And to all the children in the world and their loving families who give it their all, everyday, for their babies.

Don't Grow Too Fast, Please

Michelle Jaffery

ILLUSTRATED BY
Paula S. Wallace

CHASING WAVES BOOKS

Omaha, Nebraska

Hardcover: 978-1-7366202-1-2
Paperback: 978-1-7366202-2-9
Kindle: 978-1-7366202-3-6

Library of Congress Control Number: 2021902332
Cataloging in Publication data on file with the publisher

For more information, visit www.ChasingWavesBooks.com

Illustrations by Paula S. Wallace
Publishing services: Concierge Publishing Services, ConciergeMarketing.com

Printed in the United States of America
10 9 8 7 6 5 4 3 2 1

As the daylight starts to fade
After a lovely day together,
My heart begins to wish
You'd stay this small forever.

I brush back your hair,
And give you a squeeze,
My sweet baby,

Don't grow too fast, please.

I wrap you close and we sway,
If only we could freeze time,
I know you'll grow and leave my nest,
but you'll forever be mine.

I nuzzle your soft cheeks,
And give you a squeeze,
My sweet baby,

Don't grow too fast, please.

Do you know how much I love you?
Can you feel how much I care?
No matter where life takes you,
I'll always be right there.

I hold your tiny hands,
And give you a squeeze,
My sweet baby,

Don't grow too fast, please.

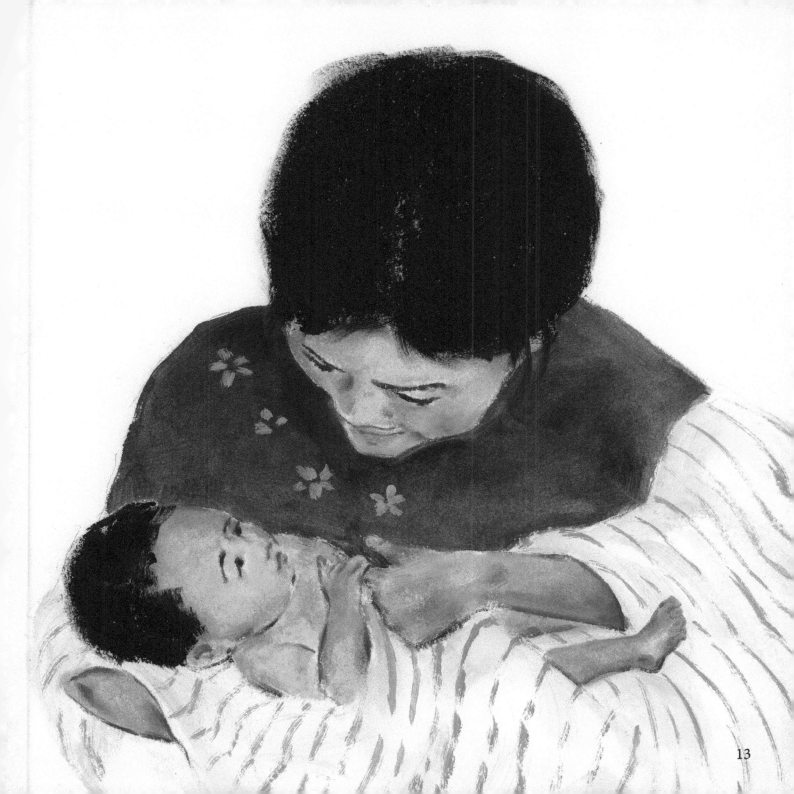

Little one, as you grow you'll learn,
life won't always be fair,
Be kind to all and tell the truth,
That's my nightly prayer.

15

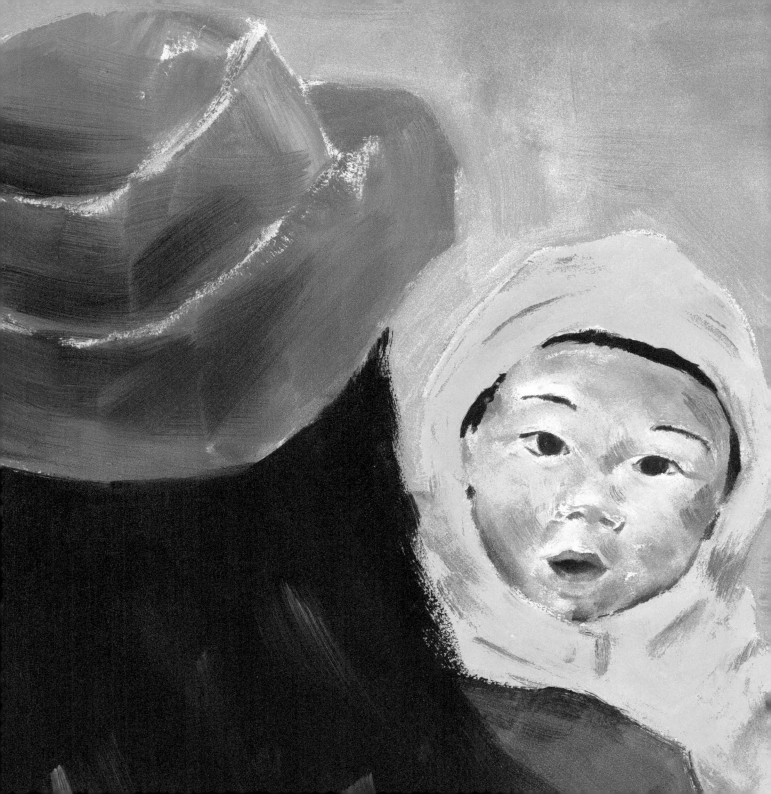

I rub your back slowly,
And give you a squeeze,
My sweet baby,

Don't grow too fast, please.

You're only this little,
For such a short while,
I soak up these moments,
and adore your sweet smile.

19

I kiss your cute head,
And give you a squeeze,
My sweet baby,

Don't grow too fast, please.

I tell myself
as you rest your head on my shoulder,
The world can wait,
Come morning you'll be another day older.

23

I read you a story,
And give you a squeeze,
My sweet baby,

Don't grow too fast, please.

In the still of the night,
'neath the glow of the moon,
Our hearts beat in sync,
It's my favorite tune.

You nod off to sleep,
after one more squeeze,
My sweet baby,

Don't grow too fast, please.

Lightning Source UK Ltd.
Milton Keynes UK
UKHW051936220221
379192UK00002B/159